For Charlie and Brian, with much love. – FW

*Dedicated to my family, and to Shelley, Bilbo and
'The Goose,' who finally got their wings.– DM*

BLOOMSBURY
CHILDREN'S
BOOKS

First published in Great Britain in 1998 by Bloomsbury Publishing Plc
38 Soho Square, London W1V 5DF

Text copyright © Fiona Waters 1998
Illustrations copyright © Danuta Mayer 1998
The moral right of the author has been asserted

A CIP catalogue record for this book is available from the British Library
ISBN 0 7475 3904 9

Printed and bound in Belgium by Proost NV, Turnhout

1 3 5 7 9 10 8 6 4 2

BLOOMSBURY CHILDREN'S CLASSICS

The Brave Sister

A Story from the Arabian Nights

Retold by Fiona Waters and illustrated by Danuta Mayer

BLOOMSBURY CHILDREN'S BOOKS

Once upon a time when magic still worked, Persia was ruled by a sultan who was a good and wise man, much loved by his people. He liked to find out for himself just what was happening in his country so at night he and his trusted grand-vizir would disguise themselves as ordinary citizens and wander the city streets, listening and watching. On just such a night it happened that, peeping through an open window, they came across three sisters earnestly discussing what sort of man they each wished to marry.

'I should like to marry the Sultan's baker. Just think of being able to eat as much of that delicious bread as I could want,' said the eldest of the sisters, who was not only greedy but rather stupid as well.

'Oh, pooh!' said the second sister. 'Why settle for the baker? I should like to marry the Sultan's cook. Then I could eat his delicious bread and his marvellous puddings.' She had a very sweet tooth but not a very sweet disposition.

And now the youngest sister spoke.

'Dear me!' she said laughing. 'I would aim much higher than that. I should like to marry the Sultan himself!'

Now the Sultan was greatly amused by what he had heard. As they crept away from the window he asked the grand-vizir to make arrangements for the sisters to attend his court the very next day.

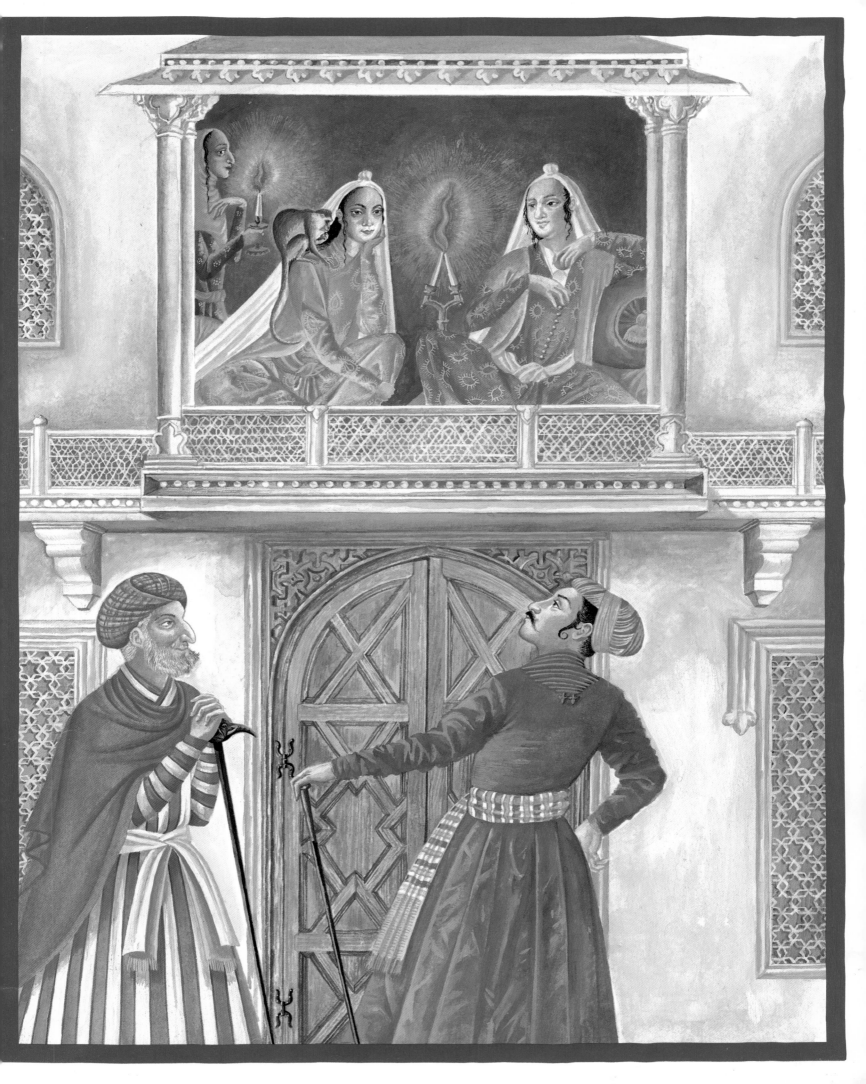

The next day the sisters were taken before the Sultan, greatly puzzled as to why he could want to see them.

'Tell me, do you remember what you all wished for last night when you were discussing your future husband?' he asked gravely.

The sisters were thrown into considerable confusion at his words, especially the youngest who blushed deeply. All three remained silent.

The Sultan continued, addressing the eldest two, 'You shall be married to my baker and my cook this very afternoon.' And turning to the youngest, whose beauty and modesty had not failed to make an impression on him he said, 'You too shall achieve your heart's desire today.'

As the Sultan finished speaking the youngest sister flung herself at his feet and stammered,

'My Lord, my foolish words should not be taken seriously. I am utterly unworthy of the honour you propose to do me, and I can only beg for your forgiveness.'

But the Sultan was not to be swayed. He was greatly taken with the youngest sister and if the truth were to be told, he was lonely in his great palace with only the grand-vizir for company.

So the three weddings took
place that afternoon. The youngest sister was
arrayed in a gorgeous dress of spun gold with fresh white orchids
in her hair. The wedding feast went on well into the night with an
endless procession of marvellous and exotic dishes and a huge cake covered in
golden sugared almonds, all prepared by the Sultan's cook and his baker, who
needless to say were not able to give much attention to their new brides.

At first all three sisters were very happy with married life at the court. But it was not long before the eldest two became jealous of all the attention paid to the youngest sister, as she was the Sultana while they were only the wives of the cook and the baker. They were determined to get their own back.

For months and months they plotted and schemed, pretending all the while to be as friendly as ever to the Sultana, but they were unable to think of a plan that would work. Then came the news that the Sultana was going to have a child.

'Now we can cause the precious Sultana some difficulty,' said the second sister, who you will remember was not a very nice person.

They never left her side until she was safely delivered of a little boy, as beautiful as the sun. The two wicked sisters stole the little baby away and set his cradle floating on the river that ran through the palace grounds. Then they told the Sultan that his beloved wife had given birth to a puppy. He was aghast but he loved his wife very much so he asked the two sisters to tell no-one of the misfortune that had befallen the Sultana.

The following year, another little prince was born and he was as beautiful as the moon. Again the wicked sisters cast the baby adrift on the river, and this time they told the Sultan that the Sultana had given birth to a kitten. He was deeply dismayed and the first seeds of doubt about his beloved wife were sown within his heart. In the third year the sisters claimed that the Sultana had given birth to a frog instead of the beautiful daughter with stars in her hair who they set, as before, on the river in her cradle. The Sultan was beside himself. He decreed that the Sultana should be banished for ever from his kingdom and he bundled her out of the palace, forbidding her ever to return. He then turned on his heel and strode into his chambers where he sat and cried and cried for he had loved his wife very much. The wicked sisters just watched.

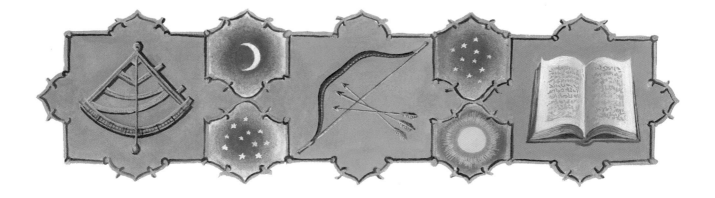

Now what, you might ask, had happened to the three children? When the prince as beautiful as the sun had been cast adrift, his cradle had been carried some way downstream through the palace gardens where it was spotted by the court astrologer. Now the astrologer was a very wise man and he realised that this was no ordinary child, so he rushed home with the baby. He and his wife had been married for many years but they had never had any children of their own so they decided to bring up the prince themselves.

The following year, by the greatest good fortune it was the astrologer who found the prince as beautiful as the moon floating down the river and once again he and his wife decided to keep the child as their own, and once again did not enquire further into the mystery. By now you will be hoping that the princess with stars in her hair was also found by the good astrologer and his wife, and so it happened, with the help of a passing genie. They gave the princes the names Bahman and Perviz after two of the ancient kings of Persia, while the princess they called Parizade, or child of the genie.

As the children grew up their gentle behaviour and good manners confirmed their high birth, and the astrologer was careful to bring them up as befitted their standing. Parizade insisted she be treated just the same way as her brothers and so she joined in all their lessons. They studied history, geography, poetry, science and art with the best teachers in the land and learned to ride, to shoot with a bow and arrow and throw a javelin. The astrologer built a splendid house in the country and there he planted the most beautiful gardens. And so they grew up together in great peace and contentment.

Time passed and both the astrologer and his wife died, without revealing to the children the strange secret surrounding their origins. It seemed as if the princes and the princess would never know of their noble birth as they lived their lives quietly in their beautiful home, far away from the bustle and intrigues of the court. But the fates intervened.

An old woman, a travelling pilgrim, came to the house one day, begging for a crust of bread and a flask of water. As Parizade and the pilgrim sat talking together amid silken and tasselled cushions, the old woman complimented the princess with the stars in her hair on the magnificence of the sweeping gardens that stretched as far as the eye could see.

'Oh, thank you,' said the princess, 'the gardens were my late father's pride and joy and I cannot imagine anything could make them more beautiful.'

'Dear child, they are indeed outstanding but I have to confess that they lack three things if we are talking of perfection,' said the old woman.

'Whatever can they be? Do tell me and I shall make arrangements for them to be obtained immediately. I am sure my father would have wished it,' cried the princess.

'Your garden lacks firstly the magical talking bird whose glorious voice persuades all the other birds to sing in chorus. And the second is the singing tree whose leaves are never silent. Lastly is the golden water. Only a single drop is required for it to rise up into the most magnificent fountain which will never dry up.'

'But where can I find these treasures?' asked the princess.

'The talking bird, the singing tree and the golden water are all to be found on the borders of this land, towards India. If you set off on the path that passes this house and travel for twenty days you should ask the first person you will then meet for directions,' and so saying the old woman went on her way.

Parizade rushed off to find her brothers to tell them of her strange encounter with the old pilgrim. Needless to say, Bahman wanted to set off immediately to find these treasures for his sister whom he loved very dearly. But Parizade urged caution.

'We don't know if the old woman was telling the truth, and besides you might meet all kinds of danger once away from our secure home!' she implored. But no amount of entreaty could change the prince's mind.

'I promise I will be careful,' Bahman said. 'But take this knife and draw it from its sheath every day. As long as it is bright and shiny then you will know all is well with me, but should it turn rusty then you will know that I am in the greatest peril,' and so saying Bahman spurred his horse and galloped away in a cloud of dust.

For twenty days he rode hard, looking neither to the left nor the right until he saw the great mountains of India in the distance.

As he drew closer he saw an ancient old man with a long white beard that grew right down to his feet. The prince alighted from his horse and bowed low in front of the dervish, for that is who he was.

'Ancient One, may your days be long in the land and may all your wishes be granted!'

(That is the correct way to address a dervish.)

The prince continued, 'I am seeking the talking bird, the singing tree and the golden water. Can you help me find them, please?'

The dervish sighed.

'Young man, I am reluctant to send you on a path that will only lead you into the greatest danger.'

'I can face any danger,' said Bahman bravely.

'Others, many others, have spoken just as proudly and all have perished,' said the dervish firmly. 'Be warned. Turn back and do not seek to go any further.'

'I thank you for your concern, sir, but I cannot turn my back on danger. I should be forever ashamed. Please tell me how I may fulfil my quest,' entreated Bahman.

The dervish saw it was useless to try any further to dissuade him so he drew a ball from within the folds of his robes and passed it to Bahman.

'Mount your horse, throw this ball in front of you and follow where it leads. You will reach the foot of a great mountain where you must dismount and walk along a path between two great rows of black stones. You must walk steadily and never once look behind you, whatever you may hear. There will be many wailing voices, cursing you and challenging you. Ignore them all. If you falter or turn you too will become a black stone like the rest. Once you reach the mountain top you will find what you seek,' and the dervish turned away sadly.

The prince leapt onto his horse and threw the ball before him. It rolled along so speedily that Bahman had great difficulty in keeping up with it, but he clung to his horse with great determination and they eventually reached the foot of the mountain. Bahman saw the path of black stones and smiled confidently.

'Well, this does not look so difficult,' he said to himself as he dismounted and strode off down the path. But scarcely had he drawn level with the first stones than he heard a voice saying, 'Who is this ruffian coming to steal the talking bird?' Without thinking, Bahman whirled round to see who had spoken and in an instant he was turned into a great black stone.

As you might imagine, back at home Perviz and Parizade were consumed with anxiety, but each time she pulled the knife from its sheath Parizade was relieved to see it still shining brightly. But then came the day when the blade was dull and rusty and Perviz and Parizade knew some ill fate had become their brother. Parizade was inconsolable.

'I wish I had never met that old woman! It was the most unlucky hour when she came here,' and she burst into tears again.

Prince Perviz was no less upset, but he was determined to take up the quest in his brother's place. In vain did Parizade try to keep him back and at first light Perviz galloped off, following his brother's trail. Before he left he gave his sister a necklace of river pearls.

'Count these every day, my sister, and as long as they remain lustrous and pure white I am alive and all is well with me. But if they grow dull and turn black, then I have met the same fate as our brother.'

And so it happened that Perviz met the dervish in the same spot. When he had explained his quest the dervish entreated him to abandon his plans, adding that only a few days before a young man bearing a strong resemblance to himself had passed by, never to return.

'That, most noble dervish, was my brother. I am determined to succeed where he has failed!' declared Perviz as he mounted his horse once again, throwing the dervish's ball in front of him. When he reached the foot of the mountain he too looked at the path lined with the black stones and said to himself, 'I am sure I will reach the top easily!' Alas, Perviz was no more successful than Bahman. No sooner did he hear a voice cursing him for his impertinence in seeking the talking bird than he drew his sword and turned to face his accuser. In the blink of an eye he too was turned into stone.

Princess Parizade was holding the pearls the very moment Perviz drew his sword. The pearls turned black before her eyes so she realised immediately that something dreadful had happened to him. Now as we know, she was a young woman of determination and great good sense so she didn't waste too much time bewailing her brother's fate, but disguising herself as a man set off in pursuit.

On the twentieth day she reached the dervish sitting under the tree. She bowed deeply to him and asked politely if he knew where she might find the talking bird, the singing tree and the golden water.

'Young lady,' he said, (for there is no use in attempting to disguise yourself from a dervish) 'I know who you are better than you do and I can see that you too are intent on pursuing this foolish family quest. You are no more likely to succeed than your unfortunate brothers.'

'We will see about that,' thought the princess as she mounted her horse. Reluctantly, the dervish gave her a ball from the folds of his robes and Parizade galloped off. When she reached the foot of the mountain she left her horse to graze, tied her flowing scarf round her ears and strode down the path between the black stones. Of course she heard nothing of the wailing voices and was soon standing in front of the talking bird.

'Brave princess with stars in your hair, from this moment on I will serve you faithfully for I know who you are better than you do,' trilled the bird.

'I am delighted to have found you, O talking bird, but where might I find the singing tree and the golden water please?' she asked.

'If you listen very carefully you will hear the singing tree, it is just in the woods behind you. Break off a small twig and when you get home plant it very carefully in your garden. The next day you will have a fully grown tree of your own. The golden water you will find in a small spring by the roots of the singing tree,' sang the talking bird.

It was just as the bird had said. Parizade broke off a twig from the tree and filled a small flask with some of the water. With the talking bird by her side she set off down the mountain. As she drew alongside the great black stones she said to the talking bird,

'I wish I knew what had become of my two noble brothers. They set off before me to seek you but I fear they have met some ill fate.'

The bird inclined his head towards a black pitcher that stood by the side of the path.

'Take that pitcher and sprinkle some of the water you will find in it over the black rocks, then you will see what you will see.'

The princess did as she was bid and as the water touched each stone it turned into a man, and suddenly there standing in front of her were her two brothers. Great was the rejoicing as you might imagine and they set off home, with all the other rescued knights following, swearing undying allegiance to Princess Parizade. Great was the joy on the face of the ancient dervish as he beheld the princes and the princess.

'My blessings go with you for I know who you are better than you do yourselves,' he murmured as they rode on.

When they arrived home, the princess went straight into the garden and the talking bird flew high into the branches of an acacia tree. No sooner had the bird begun to sing than the garden was filled with the voices of a thousand others – larks, nightingales and thrushes.

The twig from the singing tree she planted carefully near the house and in the twinkling of an eye there stood a fully grown tree.

The golden water she poured into a great marble basin. The water bubbled and then shot high into the air, the biggest fountain ever seen.

Now such wonders are not easily kept secret and it was not long before rumours reached the palace, and then the courtiers, and finally the great Sultan himself as he sat silently in his gloomy chambers. He had not ventured outside in all the years since he banished his Sultana, but he sent a message to Bahman and Perviz and Parizade saying he would like to visit their gardens to see these great wonders. Princess Parizade felt sure the Sultan would be angry that they had made their garden more splendid than his.

'Once again, I wish I had never met that old woman. It was indeed the most unlucky hour when she came here,' she sobbed. But Bahman and Perviz entreated her to be cheerful.

'We have only heard good things of our Sultan. We should be honoured that he is coming to visit us,' and they hurried away to make the necessary preparations. The princess went sadly into the garden to speak to the talking bird, but he did not seem to share her concerns.

'It is very necessary that the Sultan should come here. You will see, everything will turn out for the best,' said the bird happily.

The day of the Sultan's state visit dawned. Prince Bahman and Prince Perviz were dressed in their finest suits of velvet with great plumes in their turbans and with golden slippers on their feet. Princess Parizade wore a simple dress of pure white silk with lots of floaty scarves and of course there were the stars in her hair.

The moment the Sultan entered the courtyard he was struck with her beauty and grace, but also with a mysterious sensation that he had met her before. And as soon as he was greeted by the two princes he was reminded of himself when much younger.

'Why, these young men could be my sons!' he mused and he sighed deeply for his beloved Sultana and his lost happiness.

The garden was a delight. Deliciously perfumed flowers brushed against their robes as the Sultan walked the paths with the princess and the princes. Great spreading trees sheltered them from the heat of the sun. Brightly coloured butterflies fluttered about their heads and gossamer dragonflies darted everywhere.

The golden water sent its great fountain
high into the air and the sun caught the rainbow lights,
sparkling as it fell back into the marble basin. The singing tree filled the
air with the sound of a thousand musicians and the Sultan felt a great peace
descend upon him. As he walked the shady paths he became aware of a great twit-
tering and chattering as if of hundreds and hundreds of birds.

'Why are there so many birds gathered here?' he asked the princess.

'My lord, it is because the talking bird who you can see there in the tamarisk tree gathers
all the birds in the air to this spot,' and she turned to the talking bird and said,

'This is the great Sultan, O talking bird. Will you welcome him to our garden?'

The bird cocked his head to one side and looked long at the Sultan.

'The Sultan is very welcome. I wish him and his descendants long life and great prosperity.'

The Sultan thanked the bird but remarked that alas, he had no children of his own.

'But the Sultan has two sons, a prince as beautiful as the sun and another as
beautiful as the moon, and he has a princess with stars in her hair as a daughter,' sang the little
bird, never taking his eyes off the Sultan.

At this the Sultan grew very pale for it was a subject that grieved him greatly as you would understand.

'What I say is true,' continued the talking bird. Your beloved Sultana bore you three beautiful children and they are all standing here beside you right now.'

And the Sultan remembered his feeling that he had seen Princess Parizade before and he remembered looking at Prince Bahman and Prince Perviz and thinking they looked like himself when much younger. And he looked again at the three young people and his eyes filled with tears as he flung his arms around them. They were indeed his long lost children!

The talking bird lost no time in telling him just how wicked the Sultana's two jealous sisters had been. The Sultan gathered his newly found children up into his great retinue and they all sped back to the palace. He sent messengers to the furthest four corners of his lands with instructions to seek out the Sultana with all possible haste.

At length word came that the Sultana had been found. The Sultan mounted his fleetest horse and galloped without pause for a day and a night until he reached the simple woodcutters' cottage where she had been living all those lost years. The Sultana came to the door, curious at all the noise outside and the Sultan slid from his horse and knelt down in front of her, begging her forgiveness. He carried her tenderly back to the palace and after she had bathed in the softest perfumed rain water and dressed in her robes of state, he presented her long lost children to her one by one. For a while nothing much was said as they just hugged and kissed each other and cried and then hugged and kissed each other all over again. And so the children came home to their rightful place beside their father, the Sultan and their mother, the Sultana. They truly lived happily ever after.

And what of the two wicked sisters? The Sultan wanted to feed them to scorpions or boil them in oil or roll them downhill in spiked barrels or chop them into little pieces and all sorts of other terrible things but the Sultana begged him to spare them. So he contented himself with making them work in the hot steamy palace kitchens with their husbands, the baker and the cook. They did not live happily ever after but grew into two very sour and ugly old crones which, of course, served them right.